A Child's First Book of

NURSERY TALES

Illustrated by
CYNDY SZEKERES

Selected and adapted by
SELMA G. LANES

A GOLDEN BOOK, NEW YORK

Western Publishing Company, Inc., Racine, Wisconsin 53404

The Little Red Hen

———◆———

Once upon a time, a little red hen was scratching in the barnyard and found some grains of wheat.

"This wheat should be planted," said she. "Who will plant these grains of wheat?"

"Not I," said the Duck.

"Not I," said the Lamb.

"Not I," said the Dog.

"Then I will," said the Little Red Hen. And she did.

When the wheat grew tall and yellow, the Little Red Hen said, "This wheat is ready to harvest. Who will cut the wheat?"

"Not I," said the Duck.

"Not I," said the Lamb.

"Not I," said the Dog.

"Then I will," said the Little Red Hen. And she did.

When the wheat was cut, the Little Red Hen said, "Now the seeds must be separated from the stems. Who will thresh the wheat?"

"Not I," said the Duck.

"Not I," said the Lamb.

"Not I," said the Dog.

"Then I will," said the Little Red Hen. And she did.

When the wheat was threshed, the Little Red Hen said, "This wheat should be ground into flour. Who will take this wheat to the miller?"

"Not I," said the Duck.

"Not I," said the Lamb.

"Not I," said the Dog.

"Then I will," said the Little Red Hen. And she did.

After the wheat was ground into flour, the Little Red Hen said, "This flour should be made into dough and baked into bread. Who will bake the bread?"

"Not I," said the Duck.

"Not I," said the Lamb.

"Not I," said the Dog.

"Then I will," said the Little Red Hen. And she did.

When the bread was baked, the Little Red Hen said, "This warm bread should be eaten. Who will eat this bread?"

"I will," said the Duck.

"I will," said the Lamb.

"I will," said the Dog.

"No, not you," said the Little Red Hen. "I will eat this bread." And she did.

The Three Little Pigs

Once upon a time, there were three little pigs who went out into the world to seek their fortunes.

The first little pig met a man with a bundle of straw. "Please, sir," he said, "will you give me some straw to build myself a house?"

The man did, and the little pig built himself a house of straw.

By and by, along came a wolf who knocked at the door and said, "LITTLE PIG, LITTLE PIG, LET ME COME IN!"

To which the pig answered, "Not by the hair of my chinny-chin-chin."

This made the wolf angry, and he said, "Then I'll huff and I'll puff and I'll blow your house in!"

So he huffed and he puffed and he blew the house in, and he ate up the first little pig.

The second little pig met a man with a stack of wood. "Please, sir," he said, "will you give me some wood to build myself a house?"

The man did, and the little pig built himself a house of wood.

By and by, along came the wolf, who knocked at the door and said, "LITTLE PIG, LITTLE PIG, LET ME COME IN!"

To which the pig answered, "Not by the hair of my chinny-chin-chin."

"Then I'll huff and I'll puff and I'll blow your house in!" snarled the wolf.

Well, he huffed and he puffed, and he puffed and he huffed, and he blew the house in. Then he ate up the second little pig.

The third little pig met a man with a load of bricks. "Please, sir," he said, "will you give me some bricks to build myself a house?"

The man did, and the little pig built himself a house of bricks.

By and by, along came the wolf, who knocked at the door and said, "LITTLE PIG, LITTLE PIG, LET ME COME IN!"

"Not by the hair of my chinny-chin-chin," said the third little pig.

"Then I'll huff and I'll puff and I'll blow your house in!"

Well, that wolf, he huffed and he puffed, and he puffed and he huffed, and he huffed and he puffed some more. But he could not blow the brick house in.

So the sly wolf said, "Little pig, I know where there is a field full of sweet turnips."

"Where?" asked the little pig.

"At Farmer Smith's. If you'll be ready tomorrow morning at six o'clock, we can go together and get some for dinner."

Next morning, the little pig got up at five o'clock and was back home with sweet turnips for his dinner before the wolf even came by.

When the wolf discovered that he had been tricked, he was angrier than ever. Still, he said in a friendly way, "Little pig, I know where there is a tree full of ripe red apples."

"Where?" asked the little pig.

"Down at Merry Garden. Tomorrow morning I will come by at five o'clock, and we can go pick some together."

This time the pig got up at four o'clock and had picked almost a basketful of ripe red apples when he saw the wolf coming. The little pig was frightened.

"What, here already?" said the wolf, licking his chops. "Are the apples tasty?"

"Delicious!" said the little pig. "Try one." And he threw an apple so far that, while the wolf chased after it, the pig was able to jump down from the tree and run home.

The wolf howled with rage.

But, next day, he came again and said, "Little pig, there is a fair at Shanklin this afternoon. Let's go together at three o'clock."

At one o'clock the little pig ran off to the fair, where he bought himself a big wooden butter churn. He was carrying it home when suddenly he saw the wolf coming. Quick as a wink, the pig jumped inside the churn to hide. By accident, he turned it over, and, bumpety-bump, the churn rolled down the hill right toward the wolf.

The wolf was so frightened by the strange object that he ran home without even going to the fair.

Later he went by the pig's house to tell him about the scary thing that had chased him down the hill.

The little pig laughed. "That was the butter churn I bought at the fair," he said, "with me inside it."

The wolf was so angry that he decided to eat up the little pig right then and there. "I will go down the chimney," he said to himself. But the little pig heard the wolf clumping up onto his roof and hung a pot full of water in the fireplace. Then he lit a blazing fire beneath it.

As the wolf started down the chimney, the pig lifted the cover of the pot. *Plop!* The wolf fell into the boiling water, and that was the end of him. As for the little pig, he didn't miss the wicked wolf one bit.

The Two Frogs

Once upon a time, there were two frogs. One lived in a mud hole near the port city of Southampton, England. The other lived in a clear pond in the capital city of London.

The two frogs lived far apart, and neither knew that the other existed. Yet, one morning, each had the very same thought—to see something of the great wide world.

So, on the same day, both started out from opposite ends of the long road connecting Southampton and London.

"Hip, hop. Hippety-hop," croaked the Southampton frog. "I'll hop right to London before I stop."

"Hop, hip. Hoppety-hip," croaked the London frog. "I'll reach Southampton my very first trip."

The way was longer and harder than either frog had expected. On and on they hopped. Hop, hip, hoppety-hip. Hip, hop, hippety-hop.

At last they came to opposite sides of the very same high hill. "Hip, hop," croaked each frog wearily. "I'll have to reach that mountain top." It took them one thousand hops each to get to the top. The frogs were astonished to see one another.

"Hello, there!" said the Southampton frog. "Where do you come from and where are you going?"

"Hello to you!" replied the London frog. "I come from the capital city and am on my way to visit Southampton."

"What a coincidence!" said the first frog. "I come from that port city and am on my way to see London!"

They sat down to rest. "It's a tiring trip," said the Southampton frog with a sigh. "If I could just catch sight of where I am going, the rest of the journey might seem easier."

"If only we were taller," said the London frog, "we might be able to see both cities from this high mountain."

"We could make ourselves taller," said the Southampton frog, "by standing on our hind legs and holding on to each other's shoulders for balance. Then we could lift our heads way up and see the cities we are traveling to."

So the London frog and the Southampton frog jumped up on their hind legs and held on to each other's shoulders. The Southampton frog was facing toward London, and the London frog toward Southampton. However, the foolish creatures forgot that, in this strange position, their great, bulgy eyes would see backward instead of forward. Although their bodies faced the cities to which they were traveling, their pop-eyes looked right back at the cities from which they had come.

"Amazing!" cried the Southampton frog. "London looks exactly like Southampton. It is hardly worth the bother to visit."

"Incredible!" said the London frog. "Southampton is the twin of London. I may just as well go home."

So both frogs turned around and hopped back to their own cities. Hippety-hop, hoppety-hip. And they lived happily ever after, each believing that the port city of Southampton and the capital city of London—which are very different places indeed—were as alike as two lily pads in a frog pond.

The Three Little Kittens

Once upon a time, there were three little kittens who lived with their mother in a snug little cottage.

When winter came with its cold and snow, Mother Cat knitted three pairs of mittens. She wanted the three little kittens' paws to stay warm.

The first pair of mittens was bright red. The second pair was pale green, and the third was deep blue. The three little kittens put on their mittens and ran outside to play.

"Be good little kittens. Don't lose your mittens!" called Mother Cat. "I shall bake a pie."

First the three little kittens threw snowballs. Next they rolled a big snowcat, and then they made kitten angels by falling backwards into the soft, white snow.

The first little kitten had very wet mittens, so he took them off and hung them on a branch to dry.

The second little kitten saw a feather in the snow and pulled off his mittens to pick it up.

The third little kitten needed her sharp claws to climb a tree and chase a bird, so she dropped her mittens by the tree trunk.

The bird flew away, but the kitten in the tree looked all around at the world beneath her. In the distance she saw a big brown dog. The dog was heading toward the three of them! The kitten scrambled down the tree to warn her brothers, and the three little kittens ran lickety-split home.

Mother Cat was waiting. "Just in time for warm pie and milk, my pets," she said. Then she saw that the three little kittens had no mittens. The kittens looked at their paws.

The three little kittens,
  They lost their mittens,
And they began to cry,
  "Oh Mommy dear,
  We sadly fear
Our mittens we have lost!"

"What! Lost your mittens?
  You naughty kittens!
Then you shall have no pie."

Miew, miew. Miew, miew.
"No, you shall have no pie."

The three little kittens went to look for their mittens. They hunted high and low. The first little kitten saw his red mittens hanging on the branch. The second little kitten found his green mittens half-buried in the snow. The third little kitten spied her blue mittens lying at the bottom of the tree.

The three little kittens,
　They found their mittens,
And they began to shout,
　"Oh Mommy dear,
　See here! See here!
　Our mittens we have found."

"What! Found your mittens?
　You darling kittens!
　Then you shall have some pie."

　Purr, purr. Purr, purr.
"Yes, you shall have some pie."

So the three little kittens sat down to eat delicious slices of apple pie.
But they were so hungry that they forgot to take off their mittens!

The three little kittens,
　They wore their mittens,
And soon ate up the pie.
　"Oh Mommy dear,
　We greatly fear
　Our mittens we have soiled."

"What! Soiled your mittens?
　You careless kittens!"
　Then they began to sigh.

　Miew, miew. Miew, miew.
Yes, they began to sigh.

The three little kittens filled the washtub with soapy water. Then they rubbed their mittens and scrubbed their mittens until they were as clean as clean could be.

The three little kittens,
 They washed their mittens,
And hung them up to dry.
 "Oh Mommy dear,
 Look here! Look here!
Our mittens we have washed."

"What! Washed your mittens?
 You helpful kittens.
But I smell a rat close by."

Miew, miew. Hush! Hush!
"I smell a rat close by."

For the rest of the winter, right up to the first warm day of spring, the three little kittens took good care of their mittens. They didn't lose them or soil them again. Purr, purr. Purr, purr.

The Three Bears

Once upon a time, there were three bears: a Great Big Bear, a Middle-sized Bear, and a Wee Small Bear. They lived deep in the forest in a house all their own.

Every morning the three bears cooked hot porridge for their breakfast. While the porridge cooled, they went out for a walk.

One day a little girl named Goldilocks, who lived on the far side of the forest, came upon their house and peeked inside.

Seeing nobody home, she tried the door. It wasn't locked, so Goldilocks went inside.

She was hungry, and when she saw three bowls of porridge on the kitchen table, Goldilocks was as happy as she could be. First she tasted the porridge in the Great Big Bowl, but it was too hot. Next she tasted the porridge in the Middle-sized Bowl, but it was too cold. Then she tasted the porridge in the Wee Small Bowl—and it was just right. So she ate it all up.

Goldilocks had walked a long way and felt tired. When she saw three chairs in the next room, she was as happy as she could be. First she tried the Great Big Chair, but it was too hard. Next she tried the Middle-sized Chair, but it was too soft. Then she tried the Wee Small Chair— and it felt just right. But Goldilocks was too heavy for it, and the chair broke all to pieces.

Feeling sleepy, Goldilocks went into the bedroom. There she found three beds side by side, and she was as happy as she could be. First she tried the Great Big Bed, but it was too hard. Next she tried the Middle-sized Bed, but it was too soft. Then she tried the Wee Small Bed—and it was just right. So she fell fast asleep.

Now the three bears came home to eat their breakfast. When the Great Big Bear found a spoon in his porridge, he roared in his Great Big Voice, **"SOMEBODY HAS BEEN EATING MY PORRIDGE!"**

Then the Middle-sized Bear saw a spoon in her porridge, and she cried out in her Middle-sized Voice, "SOMEBODY HAS BEEN EATING MY PORRIDGE!"

When the Wee Small Bear looked at his empty bowl, he squeaked in his Wee Small Voice, "SOMEBODY HAS BEEN EATING MY PORRIDGE—AND IT'S ALL GONE!"

So the three bears began to look about. When the Great Big Bear looked at his armchair, he found the cushion out of place. He roared in his Great Big Voice, **"SOMEBODY HAS BEEN SITTING IN MY CHAIR!"**

When the Middle-sized Bear looked at her armchair, she found the pillow on the floor. So she complained in her Middle-sized Voice, "SOMEBODY HAS BEEN SITTING IN MY CHAIR!"

Then the Wee Small Bear looked at his chair and cried out, "SOMEBODY HAS BEEN SITTING IN MY CHAIR—AND IT'S BROKEN ALL TO PIECES!"

Next the three bears went into the bedroom. When the Great Big Bear found his bolster out of place, he roared in his Great Big Voice, **"SOMEBODY HAS BEEN LYING IN MY BED!"**

When the Middle-sized Bear found her blankets mussed, she said in her Middle-sized Voice, "SOMEBODY HAS BEEN LYING IN MY BED!"

Then the Wee Small Bear looked at his bed and cried out, "SOMEBODY HAS BEEN LYING IN MY BED — AND HERE SHE IS!"

So shrill was the voice of the Wee Small Bear that Goldilocks awoke at once. When she saw the three bears looking at her, she was as frightened as she could be. She leapt out of the bed, jumped through the low, open window, and ran home as fast as her legs could carry her.

The three bears never ever saw Goldilocks again.

Chicken Little

Once upon a time, Chicken Little was pecking at some corn in the barnyard when—*whack!*—an acorn fell on her head.

"Goodness gracious!" thought Chicken Little. "The sky is falling down. I must run and tell the king."

So Chicken Little went along and went along until she met Henny Penny. "Where are you rushing?" clucked Henny Penny.

"Oh! I'm running to tell the king that the sky is falling down," peeped Chicken Little.

"Dear me!" said Henny Penny. "May I come too?" So Henny Penny and Chicken Little ran to tell the king the sky was falling down.

They went along and went along until they met Cocky Locky. "Where are you two rushing?" crowed Cocky Locky.

"Oh! We're running to tell the king that the sky is falling down," said Chicken Little and Henny Penny.

"My, oh my!" said Cocky Locky. "May I come too?" So Cocky Locky, Henny Penny, and Chicken Little ran to tell the king the sky was falling down.

They went along and went along until they met Ducky Daddles. "Where are you three rushing?" quacked Ducky Daddles.

"Oh! We're running to tell the king that the sky is falling down," said Chicken Little, Henny Penny, and Cocky Locky.

"Great heavens!" said Ducky Daddles. "May I come too?" So Ducky Daddles, Cocky Locky, Henny Penny, and Chicken Little ran to tell the king the sky was falling down.

They went along and went along until they met Goosey Poosey. "Where are you four rushing?" honked Goosey Poosey.

"Oh! We're running to tell the king that the sky is falling down," said Chicken Little, Henny Penny, Cocky Locky, and Ducky Daddles.

"For goodness sakes!" said Goosey Poosey. "May I come too?" So Goosey Poosey, Ducky Daddles, Cocky Locky, Henny Penny, and Chicken Little ran to tell the king the sky was falling down.

They went along and went along until they met Turkey Lurkey. "Where are you five rushing?" gobbled Turkey Lurkey.

"Oh! We're running to tell the king that the sky is falling down," said Chicken Little, Henny Penny, Cocky Locky, Ducky Daddles, and Goosey Poosey.

"Dreadful!" said Turkey Lurkey. "May I come too?" So Turkey Lurkey, Goosey Poosey, Ducky Daddles, Cocky Locky, Henny Penny, and Chicken Little ran to tell the king the sky was falling down.

They went along and went along until they met Foxy Woxy. "Where are you six rushing?" barked Foxy Woxy.

"Oh! We're running to tell the king that the sky is falling down," said Chicken Little, Henny Penny, Cocky Locky, Ducky Daddles, Goosey Poosey, and Turkey Lurkey.

"Why didn't you come straight to me?" said Foxy Woxy. "I know a shortcut to the king's palace. Just follow me."

"Oh, yes, most certainly," said Chicken Little, Henny Penny, Cocky Locky, Ducky Daddles, Goosey Poosey, and Turkey Lurkey.

So Turkey Lurkey, Goosey Poosey, Ducky Daddles, Cocky Locky, Henny Penny, and Chicken Little all followed Foxy Woxy.

They went along and went along until they came to a narrow, dark hole. Now this was the door to Foxy Woxy's den. But Foxy Woxy said, "Here we are. The best shortcut to the king's palace. Just follow me."

"Oh, yes, most certainly, right away," said Chicken Little, Henny Penny, Cocky Locky, Ducky Daddles, Goosey Poosey, and Turkey Lurkey.

So Foxy Woxy ran into his den, but he didn't go far. He turned and waited in the dark for the others. First Turkey Lurkey appeared. *Whump!* Foxy Woxy knocked Turkey Lurkey on the head and threw him over his shoulder to roast for supper. Next came Goosey Poosey. *Thump!* Down she went, and Foxy Woxy threw her over his shoulder. So it went with Ducky Daddles and Cocky Locky. But before Foxy Woxy could reach Henny Penny, she cried out a warning to Chicken Little.

So Chicken Little turned her tail feathers and ran back to the barnyard as fast as her legs could carry her. She was so glad to be home that she never again tried to tell the king anything at all.

The Wolf and the Seven Little Kids

———◦◦———

Once upon a time, a mother goat had seven little kids whom she loved with all her heart. One spring morning she decided to go out into the field to gather tender green sprouts for her kids' supper. She picked up her basket and called the seven kids to her side.

"While I am gone," she said, "be sure to keep the door locked; open it for no one. Be especially careful of the clever wolf. He will try to fool you, but you can always recognize him by his rough voice and his black feet."

"Don't worry, dear Mother," bleated the kids. "We'll take care." So the mother goat went on her way with an easy mind.

Soon there came a knock at the door. A rough voice said, "Lift the latch, my dears. Mother is home and she's brought you each a present."

But the seven kids remembered what their mother had told them. "We will not open the door," they cried. "Our mother has a sweet voice. Yours is as rough as sandpaper. You are the wolf! Go away!"

So the crafty wolf ran to the grocer and bought a pot of honey. He licked it all up to make his voice sweet. Then he went back to the house of the seven little kids.

This time he knocked and said sweetly, "Lift the latch, my darlings. Mother is back with presents for you all." But the wolf had leaned a big black paw against the window, and the kids remembered what their mother had told them.

"We will not open the door," they cried. "Our mother has lovely white feet. Yours are black as coal. You are the wolf! Go away!"

Now the wolf ran straight to the baker. "Put white flour on my feet," he said, "or I will eat you up!" The frightened baker did as he was told, and the wolf walked with care back to the house of the seven little kids.

Gently he knocked, then sweetly said, "Lift the latch, my own dear goatlets. Mother is home at last, with presents for one and all."

"First show us your feet," said the cautious kids. The clever wolf held two flour-covered paws up to the window. Since the paws were white, the seven kids felt sure it was their mother. They lifted the latch and opened the door.

In bounded the wolf, and the little kids all ran to hide. One dived under the table; a second hid beneath the bed covers; a third crouched behind the stove; a fourth squeezed under the sink, a fifth into the cupboard, and a sixth beside the washbowl. The youngest kid sprang into the clock case.

The wolf found them and gobbled them up, one right after the other —except for the smallest kid hiding in the clock case. Then, being quite full, the wolf went outside to take a nap.

When the mother goat came home, what a sight met her eyes! The house door was wide open; the furniture lay this way and that; the quilt had been ripped from the bed; and the washbowl lay broken to pieces. She looked for her dear children, but they were nowhere to be found. In tears, she called to them. There was no answer—except for the little voice of the youngest kid.

"I am in the clock case, dear Mother," he whispered. She took the frightened kid out and kissed him tenderly. He told her how the wolf had fooled them and had eaten all his brothers and sisters. The mother goat wept bitterly.

Unable to stay in the sad house a moment longer, she went outside. Then she heard the wolf snoring. Looking closely at the monster, she saw his fat belly moving. "Mercy me!" she said. "Can my poor children still be alive?"

She sent the littlest kid to fetch her scissors, a needle, and some thread. Then the mother goat cut open the cruel beast's stomach. No sooner had she made a small opening than one little kid's head popped out. She cut a bit more and all six kids leapt out, one after the other.

The little kids weren't hurt at all because the greedy wolf had swallowed them whole. What a joyous reunion they had with their mother!

Then the mother goat said, "Quickly, children. Find some big stones. We will put them in the wicked wolf's stomach while he is still asleep." This they did, and the mother goat sewed him up again.

When the wolf awoke, he felt thirsty. He stood up, which was not easy with all those rocks inside him, and walked to a nearby stream. As he bent over to drink, the heavy stones toppled the wolf right into the water, where he drowned.

The seven kids were watching and cried aloud, "The wicked wolf will bother us no more!" With their mother, they gathered in a circle, and all danced for joy.

The Town Mouse and the Country Mouse

Once upon a time, a country mouse invited his cousin, a town mouse, to visit him in the green meadow where he lived.

The Town Mouse came wearing an elegant suit and a beautiful polka-dot neckerchief. The Country Mouse set out the most elegant dinner he could offer: toasted barley seeds, kernels of fresh corn, vegetable roots, and pure spring water to drink. For dessert, there were wild blackberries.

But the Town Mouse didn't think much of this simple meal. After the two had eaten the last juicy berry, he turned to the Country Mouse and said, "Poor cousin! In this rustic place, you live no better than the ants or beetles. Come to town with me. I promise you will dine like a king."

So the Country Mouse agreed to go with the Town Mouse for a visit. The trip was long, and the cousins arrived after dark at a splendid house. It was brightly lit, as if by ten thousand fireflies.

Once inside, the Town Mouse led his cousin to a pantry filled with wondrous treats. On a wooden counter were tender bacon rinds, crumbs of rare cheeses, potato peelings, bits of soft butter, and several drops of wine in the bottoms of glasses.

The Country Mouse could scarcely believe his eyes. But no sooner had he begun to nibble than heavy footsteps approached. The pantry door swung open. "It's the cook!" whispered the Town Mouse. "Quick. Follow me." The cousins scampered off to hide in a small, uncomfortable hole.

When all was quiet, the Town Mouse took his frightened cousin back to the feast. The Country Mouse was about to swallow a tidbit of sponge cake when the pantry door opened again — this time slowly and softly. "Hah! The cat," said the Town Mouse, and the cousins scuttled for the safety of the cramped mouse hole.

At last the cat was gone, and the Town Mouse urged his cousin to finish his dinner. But the trembling Country Mouse had lost his appetite. He bade his cousin a hasty good-bye. "Your house is lovely and the food delectable," he said. "But, for me, I prefer to nibble my barley seeds and vegetable roots in the peace and quiet of a green meadow."

From that time on, though they exchanged Christmas and birthday cards, neither the Country Mouse nor the Town Mouse ever felt the need to visit each other again.